Check out the 5 Lords of Pain
website:

www.fivelordsofpain.co.uk

For amazing downloads, behind-the-
scenes action and exclusive extracts
from the next books ...

The 5 Lords of Pain Books

THE
LORD
OF
TEARS

by

JAMES LOVEGROVE

The 5 Lords of Pain
Book 3

First published in 2010 in Great Britain by
Barrington Stoke Ltd
18 Walker Street, Edinburgh, EH3 7LP

www.barringtonstoke.co.uk

ISBN: 978-1-84299-815-1

Printed in Great Britain by Bell & Bain Ltd

Contents

The Story So Far

The Contest takes place every 30 years. It's a series of duels between five demons and a single human champion. What's at stake is nothing less than the fate of the world.

The human champion is always a member of the Yamada family. The task of defeating the demons, who are known as the Five Lords of Pain, is passed down from father to son. It has been that way for many hundreds of years.

Tom Yamada is the latest in line to face the Five Lords. Tom is only fifteen, and his Contest isn't due to start until he is 30. But something has gone wrong. Now Tom finds himself having to fight the duels too early.

Tom has won the first two duels. He has defeated the Lord of the Mountain and the Lord of the Void. Tom's mother and his martial arts trainer, Dragon, are thankful.

During the second duel, however, Tom was badly hurt.

Now his best friend Sharif has become the victim of a mystery attack, and Tom has travelled to Japan, seeking revenge ...

Chapter 1
A Park in Tokyo

It was getting late. The sun was going down behind the sky-scrapers of Tokyo. The shadows were growing long in the district of Harajuku, where Tom was waiting.

Tom looked around, trying to spot the figure dressed in white. He'd seen it the night before. If the figure was what he thought it was, he was sure it would be back tonight.

Tom had been in Tokyo for two weeks. He'd spent the time hanging around in public areas of the city, places where he would get noticed. He was not trying to hide the fact that he was there. Indeed, he'd been trying to stand out, trying to make people notice him. He wanted to be spotted. He wanted to be found.

Then yesterday evening, in the Harajuku district, it had happened. He'd caught sight of a white figure watching him from some way off.

Harajuku was where lots of the local kids got together, dressed up as people from the worlds of manga, movies and music. They liked to walk around, looking at each other's costumes. Tom had seen super-heroes such as Spider-Man and Superman. He'd also seen girls dressed as Sailor Moon and boys dressed like the death god Ryuk from *Death Note*. There'd been robots, rock stars and any number of street dancers and performers. It was crazy, like a cross between a meeting of sci-fi fans and a talent show.

At first the white figure had just seemed to Tom like just another kid in a costume, one who happened to be dressed like a ninja.

That was why no one else paid much notice to the white figure. But the white figure kept staring at Tom … and he looked just how Tom had been told a Shinobi Ghost would look. His head was wrapped in a long scarf which acted as both hood and mask. His whole face was covered except for the eyes. And his eyes were pale and empty. White.

Like the eyes of a dead man.

At last Tom made a move towards him. Then some people walked between him and the white figure. After they'd passed by, the white figure was gone.

That was when Tom knew it must have been a real Shinobi Ghost. He stayed on in Harajuku till midnight, but didn't see the Shinobi Ghost again.

The next night, he returned to Harajuku. He was certain the Shinobi Ghost would come again.

He was right. Just as darkness fell, the Shinobi Ghost appeared. He was standing next to the entrance to a park called Yoyogi Park. Tom ran towards him, pushing his way through the crowds. But the Shinobi Ghost had vanished by the time Tom reached the park entrance.

That didn't matter. Tom knew he was meant to go into the park. The Shinobi Ghost had wanted Tom to see him and was inviting Tom to follow him.

Tom walked along the paths that ran between the park's lawns. Lamps were on, giving out a dim orange glow. The trees were black against the sky. Two women jogged past him. They chatted as they ran, their voices as musical as birds. Everyone seemed to be going the other way from Tom. People were leaving the park. Soon Tom would be there on his own. That was how he wanted it. Just him, and the Shinobi Ghost.

It was Dragon who had first told Tom about the Shinobi Ghosts. He'd said that no one could be sure they really existed. They were Japan's best-kept secret. Most Japanese people hadn't even heard of them.

They were ninja assassins, trained killers, and not just any old ninja assassins either.

The Shinobi Ghosts were *dead* ninja assassins. They had been brought back to life and given magical ninja skills.

"Zombie ninjas?" Tom had said when Dragon had told him this. "You've got to be kidding!"

"That's why no one believes the Shinobi Ghosts are real," Dragon had replied. "Dead bodies given life again through magic and turned into masters of evil and murder. Isn't that too strange to be true? And yet it *is* true, or so I've been told."

"And it's one of these Shinobi Ghosts who put my friend Sharif in hospital?"

"I think so. That's what it looks like."

Not long ago, Sharif had been attacked on his own front doorstep, in the day-time. He had been stabbed more than twenty times.

And no one had seen a thing.

The street had been busy at the time. People had been leaving their homes to go to work. There'd been quite a lot of traffic on the road. Sharif's screams had been heard, but no one had seen anyone running away from the scene of the crime. Nor had CCTV cameras in the area filmed anything odd or strange.

Sharif himself hadn't seen anything either. He had, it seemed, been attacked by an unseen hand. Or a ghost.

The newspapers had called it a race hate attack. They'd said it must have been skin-heads or white thugs picking on a young lad who'd done nothing wrong except to have dark skin. The police were working on the same theory. They'd been hunting for the attacker ever since, bringing in all the violent nutters in the area for questioning. They'd not yet found out who had done it.

And they never would, if Dragon was right.

Because the attacker was a Shinobi Ghost, and Shinobi Ghosts never got seen and never got found out.

Sharif was still in hospital. He was getting better. He was off the critical list, and the doctors were saying he would make a full recovery. The stab wounds had been deep, but none of them had hit Sharif's lungs or heart or any other vital organ. It was a miracle.

Tom could remember only too well his first sight of Sharif lying in a hospital bed. Tom himself was only just getting better from a stab wound at the time. His left arm had a bandage and was in a sling, and it hurt like mad.

But his wounds were not nearly as bad as his friend's. Sharif had been covered in bandages from head to toe. He looked a bit like a mummy in an old horror movie. A drip was stuck in his arm. He was linked up to a machine that kept track of his heartbeat.

And he was so still and pale as he lay there. He'd been asleep that first time Tom came to visit, and he was hardly breathing. To Tom he looked more dead than alive.

"Whoever did this, Sharif," Tom had whispered to his friend, "I'll get them. I promise you. I'll make them pay."

Now he was in Tokyo, Japan's capital city, and his plan was to do just that – make the Shinobi Ghosts pay.

Tom followed a twisting path through the park. Yoyogi Park seemed to be as big as Hyde Park in London, perhaps bigger. There were a million places to hide. The Shinobi Ghost could be anywhere.

Then Tom saw a movement to his left. Something white flitted between the trunks of two trees.

Then there was another movement, this time to his right. A pale shape glimmered near some bushes. It vanished from view the moment Tom looked right at it. He couldn't be at all sure that it had even been there.

But it *had* been there. He knew it.

So there wasn't just one Shinobi Ghost. There were at least two, and there might well be more. And they were showing themselves. They were letting Tom see them. They were letting him know that they knew he was there and that they knew *why* he was there. They were lying in wait. Any moment, they might attack.

Tom walked on. His footsteps sounded loud in the empty park.

He passed a massive concrete building. It was a gym, where the Olympic Games had been held back in the 1960s. He spotted a Shinobi Ghost prowling across its oddly shaped roof.

He walked alongside a large pond full of golden fish. A Shinobi Ghost was skulking in the shadows next to the pond.

He went past an open-air theatre. A Shinobi Ghost was standing at the edge of the stage.

Soon Tom was seeing Shinobi Ghosts everywhere. He got the feeling that they were gathering around him. They were closing in on him.

A trickle of sweat rolled down Tom's spine. The air was muggy and it was hard to breathe.

Tokyo in June was a hot place to be. Even at night, the city did not cool down. It felt like being trapped in an oven. But that wasn't why Tom was sweating.

Suddenly Tom looked round and saw a Shinobi Ghost right behind him. The Shinobi Ghost was out in the open now. He was following Tom.

More Shinobi Ghosts came into view. They moved at the same speed as Tom did. They made no sound.

They were behind Tom and on both sides of him. But not in front.

Tom knew why.

They were "herding" him, as dogs did with sheep. They were making him go where they wanted him to.

He was desperate to run away, get out of there, now. He counted at least twenty Shinobi

Ghosts. There might well be more. And he was on his own.

But he couldn't run away. He'd made that promise to Sharif. He had to see this through to the end.

In front of him he saw a temple. A huge wooden gateway stood in front of it. Tom passed through the gateway, into a large square. There were low, rather grand buildings on all sides. The largest of these was in front of Tom. It had a high roof that was held up by wooden pillars. There was no front wall. You could walk straight inside, into an open area where you could kneel and pray to the gods and leave messages for members of your family who had died.

The Shinobi Ghosts came through the gateway after Tom, then halted. They stood in a large half-circle round Tom, still keeping their distance. Tom guessed that the temple was where they wanted him to be. This was the place the Shinobi Ghosts had been herding him to.

He grew tense, waiting. Waiting for them to attack. All of the Shinobi Ghosts were armed. They were carrying every kind of ninja weapon Tom could think of.

"Come on," he muttered under his breath. "Do it. Let's get this over with. Bring it on."

Then a voice rang out from the building ahead.

"Tom Yamada!"

It was a girl's voice.

"*Konnichiwa.*"

This was a Japanese greeting.

"I don't speak Japanese," Tom said. "Only English. Who are you?"

The girl came out of the shadows between two of the building's wooden pillars. She

15

stepped into the lamp-light. She was perhaps fourteen or fifteen years old, and slim and short. Very short, in fact. Five feet tall, if that.

Her short dark hair was tied in bunches above her ears. She was wearing a bright red skirt and a white blouse. Her socks rose above her knees and her shoes were shiny black leather. She had a Hello Kitty shoulder-bag hanging by her side.

"I am Mai," she said. "Mai Yamada. Your cousin. And I have one thing to tell you, Tom. Try not to die."

Chapter 2
Shinobi Ghost Attack

Mai Yamada raised a hand and clicked her fingers.

At once, two of the Shinobi Ghosts started running at Tom.

Tom flicked both his arms. He'd been hiding a *tanto* dagger up each of his sleeves. The daggers had been held in place by loose straps. Now they slid down and he caught them by the handles.

The two Shinobi Ghosts leapt into the air. Each of them was carrying a *ninja-to*, a short ninja sword. The swords flashed in the lamp-light.

Tom set his feet firmly on the ground and held the *tanto* daggers so they pointed outwards. He slashed out at the two Shinobi Ghosts as they rushed past him on either side. Both Shinobi Ghosts fell to the ground, rolled over, and lay still.

Mai Yamada clicked her fingers again. Two more Shinobi Ghosts sprang at Tom.

Tom was trying hard not to think about the girl, Mai. A Yamada? His cousin? Tom hadn't even known he *had* a cousin. And now she wanted him dead?

But it was not safe to think when you were in the middle of a fight. The fight itself was the only thing you should focus on. Everything else had to wait.

Tom swung his daggers as the two Shinobi Ghosts closed in. They were coming at him from both sides. One had a *hanbo*, a staff with a blade at either end. The other had a *hoko*, which was a kind of three-pronged fork, with a long pole for a handle. He was holding it at waist level, like a lance.

Tom threw one of the *tanto* daggers into the face of the Shinobi Ghost who was carrying the *hoko*. The living-dead ninja came on, still charging at Tom. Tom grabbed the shaft of the *hoko* and rammed the blade end into the stomach of the other Shinobi Ghost. The *hoko* went right through the Shinobi Ghost, its three prongs jutting out from his back. Then Tom wheeled round and cut open the neck of the first Shinobi Ghost, who fell to the ground without a sound.

It wasn't killing. These ninjas were dead already. Tom thought of it as switching off a machine. A machine powered by magic.

"Shinobi Ghosts aren't alive," he recalled Dragon telling him. "Magic spells make them appear to be alive, like electricity in a robot. A wound that would kill a human will break the flow of the magic through a Shinobi Ghost's body. That is how you destroy them."

It hadn't made much sense to Tom at the time, but he'd guessed that it was good advice. And now he was doing as Dragon had said, and it was working!

More Shinobi Ghosts ran at him. Four of them this time.

Tom didn't see what their weapons were. He slipped another of his own weapons from out of his trouser pocket. This was a length of chain with weights on both ends, a *manriki-gusari*. Tom whirled it round and round. He bashed the head of one Shinobi Ghost with it, then the head of another, crushing both their skulls. He snagged it around the neck of the third of the four Shinobi Ghosts. Then, with a two-handed grip on the chain, he swung the Shinobi Ghost himself, slamming him into the

fourth. Tom plunged a *tanto* dagger into the
two ninjas' chests as they lay on the ground in
a heap. Instead of blood, a sticky black goo
oozed out. It looked a bit like tar, and it stank.

A Shinobi Ghost raised a bow and aimed an
arrow at Tom. Tom dived to one side. The
arrow zinged over his head and landed smack
in the face of a Shinobi Ghost right behind him.

Tom threw his dagger at the Shinobi Ghost
with the bow before the ninja could string a
new arrow. The Shinobi Ghost toppled over
onto his back.

Tom snatched three *shuriken* from his back
pocket. He flung the throwing-stars at three
more of the Shinobi Ghosts one after the other.
He hit them all in the throat, and they fell
clutching their necks.

There were about ten Shinobi Ghosts left
standing. They stalked towards Tom, coming
closer and closer in a smaller and smaller
circle. Tom went into a crouch, ready to

defend himself. He'd run out of his own weapons. He felt around for a *kama* sickle that lay in the hand of one of the Shinobi Ghosts he had knocked down.

"Enough!" cried Mai Yamada, clapping her hands.

The Shinobi Ghosts stood still, as stiff as statues.

"I've seen what you can do now," Mai said to Tom. "You fight well. Though you may have Western blood in you, you still have the Yamada family skills. But Shinobi Ghosts are one thing. How will you do against a *living* enemy?"

"Who do you have in mind?" Tom asked.

Mai took a step towards him.

"Me," she said.

"You want me," Tom said, "to fight *you*?" He gave a snort. "Don't be daft."

"I don't know this word 'daft'," said Mai. "But I think I can guess what it means. You're calling me stupid."

"If you like. 'Stupid' will do."

Mai gave the Shinobi Ghosts an order in Japanese. They shuffled aside, leaving her and Tom facing each other alone.

"To you I am just a silly, stupid little girl, aren't I?" she said to Tom. "Not a fighter. That's what you think?"

"Yeah," said Tom. "That's about it. You're in charge of these Shinobi Ghosts. That's a pretty cool trick. But a fighter?" He looked at Mai, and shook his head. "Nuh-uh."

"Then," said Mai, "you must think I can't do ... *this*!"

She sprang at him in a two-legged drop kick. The blow from her feet on Tom's chest knocked him right over onto his back. He lay on the ground panting, hardly able to breathe.

She's fast, Tom thought. *Very fast.*

He dragged himself to his feet.

Mai danced in circles around him, her hands up and ready.

Tom came at her. His right hand came down hard in a simple *karate* chop.

Next moment, he was flat on his back again. Mai had grabbed him and thrown him over like a sack of potatoes.

She's not just fast. She's strong, too, thought Tom.

Once more he got to his feet. He brushed himself down. He felt sore all over. And ashamed that this girl had made him look a fool.

Mai gave a cruel smile, and Tom understood that he was in for a hell of a fight. Perhaps the fight of his life.

Chapter 3
Cousin Fights Cousin

Mai went into cat stance. She held the pose so well, Tom wouldn't have been surprised if she'd started to meow.

"How long have you been studying martial arts, Tom?" she asked.

"Seven years," Tom told her proudly. He dropped into the northern position. He got down low with his right arm and right leg stuck out in front of him. He placed his left arm flat across his belly with the middle and index fingers raised.

"Only seven?" said Mai. "I began *my* training as soon as I could walk."

She lashed out with a low kick. Tom blocked it with his left hand.

But the kick was not the real attack. Mai wanted to make Tom think she was aiming at his left side, so he would forget about defending his right side. She followed the kick with a swift palm-heel punch. Tom saw it coming but couldn't duck in time. She hit him in the face, on his right cheek. Tom staggered back, stunned.

Mai moved into monkey stance. She struck out at Tom with a kind of rolling motion. Her hands were loosely curled.

Tom shook his head to clear it. He spat blood from his mouth. Mai had knocked one of his teeth loose.

He put all his weight on his back foot. He waited for Mai to get close, then hit out at her with a hammer-blow punch.

Mai stopped the punch with her hands flat and locked together like the wings of a bird. At the same time she brought her knee up and rammed it into Tom's stomach.

Tom had been ready for this, however. He bent double to avoid Mai's knee. Then he shoved her leg aside, aiming a front kick at her at the same time. His toes caught Mai under the chin. Her head snapped back.

Mai took a few steps back.

"At last," she said. "You made contact. I was beginning to think this was going to be a one-sided battle."

"Well, I may not have had as much training as you," said Tom, "but I still know a thing or two."

"We'll see, shall we?" said Mai.

She ran through a whole lot of different stances. She shifted from one to the next, her body flowing into each position. It was something special. Elegant. Mai moved like a ballet dancer, yet there was great power in her limbs too.

Tom was impressed, although he tried not to show it.

"Lovely," he said. "Tell me, do you do *walking against the wind* as well? And *trapped in a glass box?*"

Then, all at once, Mai was a human tornado. She came at Tom, firing off punches and kicks in every direction. Tom tried, but he couldn't block them all. He was banged this way and that. Mai hit him on his head, his body, his legs – all over.

At last she stopped, stepped away from him, and bowed to him in a formal manner.

Every inch of Tom felt battered. She had hit him all over. He knew how it must feel to be a punch-bag at a boxing gym.

"You came here for revenge, didn't you, Tom?" Mai said, gloating. "But you're not doing a very good job of it."

"Why did you hurt Sharif?" Tom asked. He was playing for time. He needed to recover from Mai's attack and get his breath back.

"*I* didn't hurt your friend."

"One of your Shinobi Ghosts did. Stabbed him and left him for dead."

"Well, why do you think that was? To get you to come here."

"Yeah, I thought that was it," Tom said, with a bitter tone in his voice.

"Your friend was bait in a trap," said Mai. "It was important that *you* saw the Ghost first of all, at your home. Then, when your friend

29

was attacked, you would be able to put two and two together and work out who did it. Most of the time a Shinobi Ghost is never seen, but this time we had to allow it for once."

"But Sharif has done nothing! I mean, he's got nothing to do with the Contest. He's just an ordinary kid. There was no need to drag him into this … this … whatever this is."

"He will be fine," said Mai. "The attack was well planned. A Shinobi Ghost knows just where to put his knife. He could have stabbed your friend another hundred times, and still not killed him or caused any lasting damage."

"Oh, yeah?" snorted Tom. "No lasting damage? What about the scars Sharif'll have for the rest of his life? And what about the *mental* damage? He'll be too scared now ever to set foot outside his front door again!"

Mai gave a shrug. "I'm sorry if that happens. But you had to be given a good reason to come here, Tom. And a good reason to find me and fight me. It had to be revenge. Nothing less would do. Nothing less would tear you away from the Contest."

"You know about the Contest?"

"I'm a Yamada. Of course I do."

"Then you know how important the Contest is," Tom said. "You know what's at stake. And yet you still went ahead and laid this trap for me. Which, by the way, wasn't much of a trap, since I chose to walk into it."

"Surely that makes it a brilliant trap?" said Mai.

"Whatever," said Tom. "All I'm saying is, ever heard of putting others first? The Contest decides the fate of the world. Whereas you're fighting me ... why? To prove you're better than me? Is that right?"

Mai nodded.

"Don't you think that's just a bit petty?" Tom said. "Couldn't you at least have waited till the Contest was over before starting all this?"

"But it isn't only about proving I'm a better fighter than you, Tom. It's also about the Contest itself."

"Huh?"

Mai rose up, moving into crane stance.

"It is not you who should be Contest champion," she said. "I should. There are still three duels left to fight. *I* should be the one who takes part in them, not you. I have greater skills. I am faster than you. I have studied martial arts longer. I have a far better chance of winning against the last three Lords of Pain than you do."

"But," said Tom, "if you know anything about the Contest, you'll know that it's a father-to-son thing. My father was the champion, and his father, all the way back to the first champion, Yoshiro Yamada."

"So?"

"So, that's how it works. That's how the Contest has always been. Every 30 years. The first-born son of a first-born son."

"So?" Mai said again, getting closer to Tom.

"You're not a son!" Tom blurted out. He was fed up with this stupid talk. "You're not male! You're – you're a girl!"

"What does that matter?" said Mai. "Now defend yourself."

And the fight began again.

Chapter 4
Body and Mind

It might have lasted half an hour. It might have lasted longer. Tom had lost all track of time.

All he knew was that Mai intended to win. She attacked without mercy. And she went on and on without a break.

There was no talk now. Mai didn't want to discuss things any more. All she wanted to do was fight.

As for Tom, he couldn't have talked even if he'd wanted to. He was too busy fending off

Mai's attacks and trying to get in a few blows of his own.

The two of them battled back and forth across the temple square. No one was there to see them except for the Shinobi Ghosts, who looked on with their dead white eyes – blank eyes that showed no trace of feeling of any kind.

Mai knew every fighting style Tom did, and quite a few he didn't. For a while they did *karate*. Then they grappled at close hand, judo-fashion. Then it was *aikido*, each trying to lever the other round and pin the other down. Then it was *jiu-jitsu*, a complex series of joint-locks and throws. Then Mai started using a weird, fancy version of *kung fu* that Tom had never seen before. It was floaty and snake-like. His only defence was to try a bit of Thai kick-boxing, meeting her graceful movements with brute force.

At some point Tom seemed to leave his body. He hardly felt the pain any more when Mai hit him again and again. It was as if he was outside himself, looking down. He was still in control of what he was doing, but he was watching himself fight at the same time. His muscles did what he told them, but he almost didn't have to make them, as if they were working of their own accord. He looked at Mai's moves, and his own, and could see several ways she might attack him next, and work out how he should attack in return. It was more like playing a game of chess than fighting. A battle of wits rather than a battle of blows.

Dragon had spoken about this feeling. He'd said it was the mark of a true warrior.

"The mind takes over," he'd said. "The body doesn't matter any more. You know just what you can do, what tricks you can use. Body and mind are as one. You are in the state of being which every true martial arts warrior aims to achieve. It is when you are fighting at your very best."

Tom could tell that this was true. He had never fought better than he was fighting right now. Mai was pushing him to his limits, and he was finding new skills that he did not know he had.

The trouble was, it needed more than that.

He was losing.

At first Tom had thought this was because he was holding back. Mai was so small and slim. It hadn't seemed right to use too much force with her. Mai had used Tom's self-confidence to get a few more blows past his guard than she should have done.

Tom had become less bothered about hitting her hard once he'd come to see that this would be no easy win. Not only that, it seemed that Mai was to blame for what had happened to Sharif. That in itself was a reason not to go easy on her.

Now Tom understood he could fight her as hard as he wanted. He didn't have to worry about her being a girl or anything like that. In fact, he needed to be as ruthless as she was.

It still wouldn't make any difference.

Mai was better than him.

Simple as that.

Mai knew more moves than he did. She was sharper, quicker. She was fitter. She knew just what to do and moved faster than him. If Tom dropped his guard for a split second, she struck like a snake. She had no mercy, too. She kept going for Tom's left upper arm, where the Lord of the Void had cut him. Either she knew already that he'd had a bad wound there, or she had guessed it by the way he was protecting that arm. The wound had healed, the muscles had knitted back together, but the arm was still a little stiff. It wasn't quite as nimble as it ought to be, and Tom knew he was using it less than the other arm. Mai kept aiming blows at the spot where, under his shirt sleeve, a huge, ugly red scar crossed the skin. Soon his arm was hurting almost as much as when the Lord of the Void had stabbed him during the last duel.

The fight went on and on. Mai scored painful hit after painful hit.

But Tom simply would not give up. His legs were starting to wobble. His strength was going. There wasn't an inch of him that didn't feel as if Mai had punched or kicked him there.

Even so he stood his ground and kept on fighting.

Mai was going to win, but Tom would make sure she didn't have an easy victory.

Then there came a moment when Tom couldn't lift his arms any more. They felt as if someone had tied huge blocks of stone to his hands.

And then his legs gave way. All of a sudden he was on his knees.

Mai stood in front of Tom. For the first time their faces were on the same level. Hers, if anything, was rather higher than his.

Mai looked delighted. But also sad. In her little-girl eyes Tom saw regret, as if she wished she didn't have to do what she was about to.

"Not bad, Tom," she said. "Not bad at all." Her voice seemed to be coming from the far end of a long tunnel. "But not good enough."

She bobbed her head to him, a sign of respect.

"*Sayonara*, Tom."

Then she slammed her fist into Tom's face, and Tom's world went black.

Chapter 5
Great-aunt Akiko

Tom came round in a small hospital room. The first thing he saw when he opened his eyes was Dragon's face. Dragon was sitting beside his bed, looking down at him with concern, but also anger. Tom knew the signs. The golden flecks in Dragon's eyes were dancing like flames.

"Before you say anything – " Tom croaked.

Dragon held up a hand. "Shut up. I don't want to hear it."

"But – "

"Not a word," Dragon snapped. "It's bad enough that you travelled all the way out to Japan to get payback for your friend. It's worse that I agreed to let you drag me along with you. But now *this*. I warned you against going to look for the Shinobi Ghosts. I said that no good would come of it. I told you to give up your desire for revenge and focus on the one thing that really mattered – the Contest. I came to Japan with you so that we could at least carry on with your training while we're here. I also hoped I could talk you out of looking for the Shinobi Ghosts."

Dragon gave a deep sigh.

"I see now that I was wasting my time," he said. "I should never have bothered. In fact, I should never have told you about the Shinobi Ghosts in the first place. I should have kept it to myself, and let you think that Sharif was the victim of white thugs instead. I forgot how headstrong you can be. I forgot that Tom Yamada does what he wants, and to hell with

42

the rest of us. Never mind the Contest. Never mind the possible end of the world. As long as Tom gets his own way, everything's fine."

Dragon's words were bitter.

"And now look at you," he went on. "Look what the Shinobi Ghosts did to you. No, look what you did to *yourself*. Tom, Tom, Tom ..."

"But it wasn't – " Tom began.

"Uh-uh!" said Dragon, holding up his hand again. "Save it. Save the excuses for someone who cares." He stood up. "Just lie there and get better. I'm told you should be well enough to leave the hospital in two or three days' time. When you get out, we'll see what we can do about getting you back into shape for the next duel. In the meantime, just consider how selfish you have been. Think about what the Contest means for the whole world. The Shinobi Ghosts could have killed you, Tom. You're lucky they didn't. Think about that."

Dragon went out, shutting the door firmly behind him, not quite slamming it.

A little later, a doctor came in to check on Tom. He examined Tom all over, made notes on a chart, nodded, smiled and left.

A short while after that, a policeman arrived.

"I am Officer Ito," he said. He spoke very good English, with hardly any accent. "May I please ask you a few questions about the attack on you in Yoyogi Park?"

Officer Ito told Tom that he had been found lying half-dead by one of the park-keepers yesterday morning. He said that it was clear that Tom had been set upon and beaten up by a group of thugs.

"It is sad," he said, "but such things do happen, even in a polite and well-run nation like ours. There are young people who have no respect for the law, no honour, no shame.

They do not welcome people from other countries. Nor do they like people who are only part Japanese, like you. I am sorry."

Officer Ito apologised like this more than once. Then he asked if Tom could tell him what his attackers looked like.

"I can't," Tom replied. "Really, I can't."

Officer Ito pressed him about this. Tom kept saying that he couldn't remember anything about the attack. He couldn't remember anything from the time he had first entered the park.

"Memory loss," Officer Ito said in the end. "Yes. This often happens in such cases. A blow to the head causes the mind of the victim to blank out. I'm sorry."

The policeman stayed a while longer, scribbling in a notebook. Then he left, offering Tom one last apology.

"I am sorry that your trip has been spoilt," he said. "Please do not think badly of Japan from now on."

Officer Ito seemed so upset about what had happened to Tom that Tom almost felt he should have told him the truth.

A nurse came to ask if Tom wanted anything. She gave him some pills, which turned out to be splendid at getting rid of his pain. It faded away, and he went to sleep.

He awoke with a start in the middle of the night. Someone was sitting at the end of his bed.

As his eyes got used to the dim light, Tom saw that it was a little old woman. She was dressed in a silk kimono and her glossy black hair was tied up on the top of her head in a bun. Her face was old and creased. Huge false eyelashes were stuck to her eyes, making them look like a pair of black spiders.

Then Tom noticed two other figures in the room. They were standing on either side of the door, like a pair of sentries outside a palace.

Two Shinobi Ghosts.

Tom gave a start. "Whoa!" he cried. He tried to climb quickly out of bed. He had to get out of the room!

The old woman stopped him. She laid a claw-like hand on his leg, pinning him in place. She was strong.

"Calm down, Tomeo," she said. Her voice grated, like a piece of sandpaper sanding wood.

"But those are ... they're Shinobi Ghosts!" Tom cried. He hated being called by his full Japanese name, Tomeo.

"I know. Have no fear. They are with me. I control them."

"Oh," said Tom. Somehow this did not make him feel any better. "Who are you?" he asked. "And how do you know my name?"

The old woman let out a dry, dusty cackle. "Who am I? You would know the answer to that, if your mother not fled to England with you when you were just a baby. You would know me very well and you would love me and treat me with great respect. I am your great-aunt, Tomeo. Great-aunt Akiko. Your grandfather's sister. You may call me either 'Great-aunt' or 'Akiko-san'. Whichever you prefer. You will call me that and nothing else, if you wish to stay on my good side."

Tom got the feeling that he would be wise to try and stay on Great-aunt Akiko's good side. She looked like a woman you didn't want to cross.

"Umm, nice to meet you, Akiko-san," he said.

Great-aunt Akiko studied him with her spidery eyes.

"Yes," she said after a while, nodding. "You are your father's son. No doubt about it. I see him in you."

"You knew my father?" said Tom. "What am I saying? If you're my great-aunt, of course you did."

"Of course I did," said Great-aunt Akiko. "I knew him very well. I was there when your father was born. I held my sister-in-law's hand all through her labour. I was the first person to see the baby, after the midwife. Your father was born dead, you know."

"Huh?" said Tom.

"Yes," said Great-aunt Akiko. "It was a long labour – a day and a half. His mother, your grandmother, went through great pain and suffering to give birth to him. And he was blue when he came out. He had stopped breathing

49

during the birth. He had been starved of oxygen. Doctors came. They tried to bring him back to life. They did not succeed. Their medicine and their machines failed them. But I prayed."

Great-aunt Akiko held her hands together, as if praying right now.

"I prayed to all the gods," she went on. "I begged them to allow your father to live. I told them the world needed him. The world needed its next champion."

Her hands parted.

"And my prayers were answered," she said. "The doctors gave up hope. They said there was nothing more they could do for him. But all of a sudden the baby gave a little cough. Then he began to cry. Your father was a fighter, you see, Tomeo. Even then, at the very start of his life, it was clear. A fighter. He fought for the right to live, and he won."

"Well, I'm glad he did, for my sake," said Tom. "Without him, I would never have been born."

Great-aunt Akiko gave him a stern look.

"Kenji Yamada was a great man," she said. "He was brave. He never, ever had any doubts about fighting in the Contest. He knew that it was the right thing to do. He faced up to his fate, even though he knew it might destroy him – as indeed it did. Can you say the same, Tomeo?"

"Uh, yeah. Yeah, I think so."

"And yet, look at you now. Lying in hospital. In very bad shape. And who did this to you? A girl. A girl who is half your size."

Tom felt himself blush. He hoped that Great-aunt Akiko wouldn't see this in the dark.

"My granddaughter Mai, in fact," she said. "She tells me you were a worthy foe, but still nowhere near as good as she was."

"That could be true," Tom said. "She was pretty good."

Great-aunt Akiko stiffened. "Mai is not 'pretty good'. Mai is superb! She is a perfect fighter. Her control is second to none. She is perhaps the most skilled martial arts expert in all of Japan."

"OK, OK," said Tom. He was starting to get cross. "I admit, she's better than me. But so what? I'm pretty damn good myself. I've beaten two of the Lords of Pain, and I'm not even meant to be fighting them for another fifteen years. Cut me some slack here."

"No, Tomeo," said his great-aunt. "I will not *cut you some slack*, as you put it. The Contest is happening. It is happening far too early, for reasons I do not fully understand. But still, it is happening. And losing the Contest is something which we cannot allow."

"I'm doing fine so far."

"No. You have been lucky so far. Not the same thing."

"I won my duels fair and square. I got those Element Gems back."

"From two of the least powerful Lords of Pain," said Great-aunt Akiko. "You have yet to meet the Lord of Tears or even, gods preserve us, the Lord of the Typhoon. You are simply not ready, not good enough, to win a duel with either of *them*."

"Hold on there, Akiko – "

"Akiko-san."

"Akiko," said Tom, wanting to annoy her. "Slag me off as much as you like. I don't know you, so what you think of me doesn't matter to me. But when all's said and done, I'm still the Contest champion. Nothing can change that. I inherited the job. Like it or not, that's just how it is. So you might as well make the best of it, instead of going on and on about how rubbish I am and how I'll most likely lose. Who else is going to be champion? No one. Because no one else can be."

"Mai can be," replied Great-aunt Akiko. Her lips were pressed tight together. Her spidery eyes glittered. Tom knew he had just made her very cross.

"Mai," he said, "is not the first-born son of the Yamada."

"But all the same she is a Yamada. That is not her proper family name, of course. She is my son's daughter and has my married family name, Umari. But there is Yamada blood in her, and it is strong in her veins. Mai knows this. That is why she likes to call herself Mai Yamada, not Mai Umari. *She* is the one who should be champion, not you."

"But she can't be! That's the whole point."

"Why?" said Great-aunt Akiko. "Because of the past? Because of the rules of the Contest?

But the Five Lords have come back early. They have not kept their side of the bargain, so why should we have to keep ours? Mai is the true Yamada champion, Tomeo. Not you. And I think, deep down, you know this too now. It is Mai who must fight the duels. I have been raising her to do just that. I have been supervising her training. I have done everything to make sure that Mai would be ready for the Contest long before she reached the age of 30, because I feared that you would not be up to the job."

"So – what are you here for, then?" Tom asked. He pointed at the two Shinobi Ghosts. "Have you brought them to kill me? Is that it? To get rid of me and leave the way clear for Mai? Because, I tell you, they'll have a hard time trying."

"I would never do such a thing, Tomeo," said Great-aunt Akiko. "You are still my family, in spite of everything. Still my own flesh and blood. I would not dream of killing

55

you. All I expect from you is to act in a way that will do honour to the family. Be sensible. I wish you to step aside. Give up the Contest. Let Mai take your place. That is all."

"That's all, huh?" said Tom. "And why should I do that?"

"For the good of the world," his great-aunt replied. "And," she added, "the good of those around you." Her voice dropped low. Tom could hear the menace in it, like a shark swimming below the surface of the sea. "Your friend Sharif Khan might not be so lucky next time round. And then there is your mother. She is not a blood-relative of mine. In fact, I despise her. She should never have left Japan after you were born. She should have stayed here and let us, your family, help bring you up. I told her not to go. I told her you would not be a true champion if you were not raised in the way of the Yamada clan. But your mother took no notice of me. I have not forgiven her for that."

56

"You wouldn't murder my mother," Tom hissed. "You wouldn't dare."

"Shinobi Ghosts can go anywhere," Great-aunt Akiko said. "You cannot see them coming. They may strike at any time. They are silent death. Remember that, Tomeo. Remember that well."

Chapter 6

Ringing Home

When Tom woke up the next morning, it all seemed like a dream. Had someone called Great-aunt Akiko really visited him in the night? Had she really asked him to let Mai take over the Contest, and said she would kill his mother and Sharif if he didn't? Tom wished it had been a dream. But he knew it hadn't.

He phoned his mother after breakfast. He got her to call him back, because the charges for long-distance calls on his mobile were horribly high.

"Tom, how are you doing?" his mother said. "Dragon phoned and told me you'd got into a spot of bother. I was all set to fly out and take you home, but he said not to. He said you'd be all right. Are you all right?"

"Yeah." Tom looked at himself in the mirror above the basin in the room. He was a mass of bruises. His skin was like a map of brown and purple islands. "Kind of. Mum, tell me about Great-aunt Akiko."

6,000 miles away, his mother drew a sharp breath.

"That witch," she said. "God, is she even still alive?"

"She came to see me. In the middle of the night."

Jane Yamada laughed. "That'd be just like her. I don't think Akiko goes out in the daylight. I think she'd burn to a frazzle if she did."

"I take it you're not her biggest fan."

"Hardly. Although, to be fair, I don't think she's *my* biggest fan either."

"Well, no, not really," Tom said. "She didn't have very many nice things to say about you."

"Akiko Umari is one of the reasons I left Japan," Tom's mother said. "The main reason, I'd say. I was upset about your father dying, of course, and I didn't want to stay there without him. It was his country. If I'd stayed, I'd have been reminded of him all the time. I needed to make a fresh start, and going back to England was the way to do that. But it was Akiko who really drove me away."

"By insisting you didn't go."

"Just so. Brrr. That creepy old lady. It gives me shivers just thinking about her. There's something very wrong with her. Does she still have jet-black hair? Even at her age!"

"It didn't look like her natural colour, if that's what you mean."

"A dye job. And what about her eyelashes?"

"Like a pair of tarantula spiders. Plastic ones," said Tom. "Why have you never told me about her before?"

"Why would I?" his mother replied. "You were better off not knowing Akiko even existed."

"Well, she's the one who organised the attack on Sharif," Tom said. "The Shinobi Ghost – he was working at her command."

His mother growled. "That sounds like Akiko. The woman would stop at nothing to get her own way. She's lower than a snake's shirt-buttons. I knew I was right to take you away from Japan. I didn't want you anywhere near her, getting her claws into you. I didn't want her to be running your life in any way. But now she's found you all the same, and caused you trouble. Am I right in thinking that she had Sharif stabbed just to get you to come to Japan?"

"Yes."

"All so that she could have a chat with you." Jane Yamada gave an angry growl. "If I ever get my hands on her ..."

"It was a bit more than a chat. In fact, she asked me to give up the Contest."

"What?"

"She wants her granddaughter Mai to take my place," Tom said.

"Oh, really now!" snapped his mother. "Akiko's gone too far. That's absurd. What *is* she thinking of? Her granddaughter take your place? Is she nuts? Does she know *nothing* about the Contest?"

"Thing is, Mum," Tom said, "I don't reckon it's such a bad idea."

Chapter 7

Eyes on Fire

Tom stepped out of the hospital's main entrance. He half shut his eyes against the glare of the sun.

He was on what must surely have been the busiest street on the planet. There were people *everywhere*. People rolled along the pavements in a great river. People flowed over the X-shaped road crossings. People spilled out of the doors of shops and restaurants. London, crowded though it could be, was never as crowded as this.

Wary, Tom joined the mad rush of moving bodies. He didn't really know where he was in Tokyo. He needed to find a subway station or a taxi.

He let himself get carried along by the torrent of people. He passed shops that were full of high-tech goods – the very latest gadgets, super-advanced stuff that wouldn't reach shops in the West for a couple of years. Then there were noodle bars where huge cooking-pots filled the air with steam and mouth-watering smells. There were also shops that sold all kinds of strange foods shrink-wrapped in plastic – mainly bits of fish, except they looked like the parts no one ever ate normally, the parts you were meant to cut off and throw in the bin.

At last the movement of the crowds brought Tom to a taxi stand. He climbed into the first car in line. He told the driver the name of the hotel where he and Dragon were staying. The driver nodded and set off. He wore a smart uniform and white gloves, and kept a polite silence as he steered the taxi through the thick traffic. He went at a slow speed and often stopped to let another car pull out in front of him. He never once honked his horn. Tom thought that London cabbies could learn a thing or two from the ones in Japan. Good driving, for instance. And good manners.

At the hotel, Tom took the lift to the tenth floor. He went to his own room, showered, and found some clean clothes. As he got dressed, he looked out of the window. The view was amazing. From up here, Tokyo was like a sci-fi movie city. The sky-scrapers gleamed. Electronic signs blazed on their sides, rippling with images and *kanji* symbols. Tom could even see the Tokyo Tower, a tall steel structure that was like a cross between the Eiffel Tower and *Thunderbird 3*.

Dragon had the room next to Tom's. Tom knocked on the door. There was no answer. He tried the handle anyway, in case Dragon was in the bathroom or something and hadn't heard the knock. The door opened.

The blinds were drawn. The room was dark.

"Hello?" Tom called out softly.

Then he saw Dragon, by the light coming in through the doorway. Dragon was sitting cross-legged in the middle of the floor. His hands were resting on his knees palms facing up.

Dragon was meditating. His eyes were closed and his face was a mask of complete peace. His breathing was so slow and shallow that Tom could barely see his chest move.

Dragon was deep down inside his own mind. He was in a faraway place inside himself. Tom could have yelled and stamped his feet, and Dragon would not have noticed.

Tom took a step back out of the room. He didn't want to disturb Dragon. He would look in on him a bit later. See if he'd finished meditating then.

"Tom," said Dragon. His eyes flipped open.

"Ah, yeah," said Tom. All at once he felt he might not be wanted. "I'm back. I just came to ... you know, to say hi. I did knock."

Dragon rose to his feet in one smooth motion. It was as though he was being pulled upright by an invisible rope.

"I heard," he said. "When I meditate, my mind is empty. But that doesn't mean I'm not aware of things going on around me. I knew you were here from the moment I heard you go into your room."

He stretched out his arms and flexed his fingers. Dragon had very long fingernails.

"Meditation is very soothing," he said. "You ought to try it some time, Tom. I could teach you. Meditation refreshes the mind the way a good night's sleep refreshes the body. It enables you to be at peace with yourself and with the world. It is the best way to relax."

"I prefer TV myself," Tom said. "That's how I switch off and relax. Watching TV makes me calm. Except when *The X Factor* is on. Then I want to throw a brick at the screen."

"Yes, well," said Dragon. "Perhaps I'd agree with you, if I had any idea what you were talking about. Now, how are you feeling?"

"OK. Not bad."

"Ready to resume your training? We have less than a fortnight till your next duel. We can take it easy to begin with. A few simple warm-up exercises. Then we'll run through some of the basic *kata*. The movements will help get your body into balance and let the flow of energy pass easily through your system. Nothing too hard. Child's play to someone like you."

"Yeah, Dragon, about that ..." Tom began.

This was it, the moment he'd been dreading, ever since Great-aunt Akiko's midnight visit.

"Listen," he said. "There's no easy way to say this, so I'm just going to come right out and say it. I ... I won't be needing training any more."

Dragon frowned. "Pardon? There must be something wrong with my ears. I could have sworn you just said you won't be needing training any more. But that's crazy. You'd never have said something like that."

"Yeah," said Tom. "Yeah, I did."

"Care to explain what you mean?"

Tom explained. He told Dragon about Mai, and about Great-aunt Akiko. He described how fantastic a martial artist Mai was, and explained how Akiko had been training her as back-up, to take his place in the Contest. He

69

repeated Akiko's threat about killing his mother and Sharif.

"So you see," he finished, "Mai *has* to fight the final three duels. It's the best thing. For everyone."

Dragon's frown became deeper and deeper. His face made Tom think of a storm cloud just before the first rumble of thunder and the start of a heavy rain.

"The best thing?" Dragon repeated. "The *best thing?*"

"Yes," Tom said firmly, even though he was shaking inside. "And you'd agree with me, *sensei*, if you'd seen Mai in action. Next to her I'm a beginner. A complete no-hoper. Mai's got Yamada blood in her, so the Lords of Pain should accept her as champion instead of me. They have to."

"How dare you, Tom Yamada!" Dragon burst out. "How dare you! For seven years, I've taught you. I've shared my knowledge with you. I've worked hard to give you the best training I can. And this is how you repay me!"

"I'm not doing this to get at you, Dragon. It's not something I've decided. It's just the way it has to be. I've no choice."

"Of course you have a choice," said Dragon. "There's always a choice."

"Not when the lives of people I care about are at risk."

"But if you don't fight in the Contest, the lives of everyone will be at risk. Not just your mother and Sharif. *Everyone*."

"Mai will win it."

"She isn't allowed to be in it!" Dragon yelled. "Only you are!"

"No one knows what's allowed and what isn't any more," Tom replied. "The Lords of

Pain have gone and messed with the rules, so why can't we mess with them back?"

"Coward," Dragon spat.

The word hit Tom like a slap in the face.

"No," he said, stung. "I'm no coward. I'm just someone with some common sense, that's all."

"Common sense? It isn't common sense to throw away the future of the world."

"I'm not doing that," Tom said. "I'm saving the future, if anything."

He turned on his heel. He'd had enough of all this. He wasn't going to change his mind, and Dragon wasn't going to be able to make him. It was time to leave.

"Tom," said Dragon. "We're not finished. Don't you walk out of here. Tom! Turn and face me, boy. I am your master. That's an order."

Tom took a step through the doorway, out into the passage.

"TOM!!!"

Dragon roared the name. The sheer fury in Dragon's voice made Tom look round.

What he saw made him gasp.

The pupils of Dragon's eyes were filled with a bright orange glow. They were on fire, burning. It was like looking into blazing flames through two round peepholes.

Dragon's eyes stayed that way for just one brief second. Then they were normal again. The pupils went back to being orange-brown with those golden flecks in them.

"Tom?" said Dragon. All at once the anger had gone out of his voice. Now his tone was soft, curious. "What is it? Why are you looking at me like that?"

"N-nothing," stammered Tom. "It's nothing. Really." He drew back into the passage. "Just ... just thought I ..."

"What? What did you think?"

"I'm going," said Tom. "Need a rest. Tired. 'Bye!"

He hurried to his room before Dragon could say or do anything else. He shut the door. He locked it. Then he slid the chain across.

He sat on the bed.

What had he just seen?

The more Tom thought about it, the more he felt that he might not in fact have seen anything.

Dragon's room had been very dim inside. The only light in it had been the light coming in from the passage outside. The golden flecks in Dragon's eyes had caught that light and reflected it. That was all it had been.

Dragon's eyes hadn't been on fire. They had simply flashed in the light from the passage.

It had been a trick of the light. Nothing else.

Chapter 8
Free Time

Tom checked out of the hotel early the next morning and took a taxi to the airport. He flew to London Heathrow. His mother was there to meet him when he arrived.

She looked him up and down. "You seem to be healing," she said. "Where's Dragon?"

Tom shrugged and made a mumbling "I dunno" sound.

"He wasn't on the plane with you?"

"I left him in Japan. We, er – we had a kind of falling-out. I expect you can guess why."

His mother could. "You're sure this Mai girl can replace you in the Contest?" she said.

"No idea," said Tom. "But I'm willing to let her try."

Jane Yamada still had her doubts about Tom pulling out of the Contest. But mostly she was just relieved.

"Then maybe, just maybe, we can start to have a normal life at last," she said. "Do you know, I feel like a great load has been lifted off me. And it's all thanks to Akiko. I never thought I'd have a reason to be grateful to that woman. But it seems I do now."

"You should give her a call," Tom said with a sly grin. "Tell her."

"Let's not get carried away," said his mother.

They went home, and for the next week Tom did very little. He stayed in the flat, watching TV or mucking about on his

77

computer. He spoke to Sharif on the phone.
He caught up on lost sleep. He went out for
walks. He even cooked dinner for himself and
his mother one evening. It was grilled chicken
and salad, nothing fancy. But it wasn't a
takeaway for once, or a microwave job, and his
mother was delighted. She acted as though
Gordon Ramsay, the TV chef, had stepped out
of the screen and whipped up the meal for
them.

"Gordon Ramsay," she said, licking her lips.
"Yum. What a dish. And I'm not just talking
about his food."

"Mum!" exclaimed Tom. "Eurgh! That is
wrong on so many levels."

Soon Tom's bruises had gone down. He
went to visit Sharif in the hospital. Sharif was
on the mend and in good spirits. He laughed
and joked with Tom. He bragged about his
scars, and claimed that all the nurses thought
he was brave and fancied him.

"And they're not mingers, any of them," he said. "They're pretty fit. I'm going to be taking down a lot of phone numbers before I leave."

Tom put a hand on Sharif's forehead. "Yup, you're burning up. Got a fever. Doctor, doctor, quick! This man's raving."

Sharif threw a cardboard bedpan at him.

"So how's the GCSE revision going?" he asked.

"Well, it sort of isn't," said Tom. "Mum's got me an extra year before I have to do them. I'll be taking them next year instead of this."

"Hey, and I've got out of doing them too," said Sharif. "That's not bad, is it? A pretty sweet deal. Almost makes it worth getting stabbed twenty times."

"So we'll be doing Year 11 again together."

"Happy times, Tom!"

Eight days after Tom returned from Tokyo, he bumped into Debbie Williams in the street. Tom was coming out of a newsagent's with a copy of *GamePro* and a mint Magnum. Debbie was going in. They almost bumped into each other in the doorway.

"Hey, Tom," Debbie said.

"Wuh," said Tom.

"How's it all going?"

"Wuh," said Tom again. He was struck dumb. He didn't know what to say. Debbie Williams had spoken to him. Debbie Williams, whom he had stared at with such longing in school for almost two years – Debbie Williams, who was as cute as anything, with her thin glasses and her blue eyes and her pointed chin – Debbie Williams had just *spoken to him?*

Tom was struck dumb.

"So, er," Debbie said. "Listen, Tom. A friend of mine's having a party this weekend.

Natalie? From our year? Natalie Bennett?
Her parents are going away and she's got the
house all to herself. The party won't be a big
one. Just a few of us from school. We'll be
hanging out, listening to some music, that's all.
But I thought, maybe you'd like to come along?
If you want. You don't have to. But you can if
you'd like. It'd be nice."

"Wuh," said Tom. This time, he managed to
make it sound a bit like a proper word: *yes*.

"Really?"

Tom nodded his head, hard.

Debbie looked surprised. And pleased.

"Cool," she said, and gave him Natalie's
address.

Tom walked home in a daze. It wasn't until
he reached his front door that he remembered
the Magnum he'd bought. The ice cream had
melted to a sticky brown and white goo inside
the wrapper.

81

Tom didn't mind in the least.

He'd been invited to a party. By Debbie Williams.

It was a date.

Well, OK, not quite.

But almost.

He told his mother about it when she came home from work.

She, in turn, told him that the light blue Element Gem had started to fade out.

"I went to the bank for a look," she said. "I thought the gem was due to begin fading, and so it has. But that isn't our concern any more, is it? Any of that stuff. We're free."

"We are," said Tom.

"And you've got a date," said his mother.

"Not quite."

"But as good as."

"Yeah," said Tom.

"How fantastic," said his mother. "Is she nice, this Debbie?"

"Oh, yeah."

Jane Yamada smiled. "My boy. Doing the things a boy his age should be doing." She gave him a stern look. "No funny business, mind, Tom."

"Mu-u-um."

"I mean it. You respect her. You behave like a gentleman."

"Mum, it's just a party."

"Even so. I know what teenage boys are like."

"You did once. A million years ago."

"None of your cheek, young man!" Tom's mother scolded. She was laughing.

Tom thought it was wonderful. He'd never known his mother to be this relaxed and carefree. He was glad that he'd gone to Japan. Glad that he'd had his butt kicked by Mai. Glad that Mai was going to be the Contest champion rather than him.

Everything was better now. The future was rosy.

Chapter 9
Baden-Baden

The challenge from the Lord of Tears arrived on Friday morning, the day before Natalie's party.

The toilet tank exploded. There was a loud *crack* from the bathroom, followed by the gush and gurgle of water splashing everywhere. Tom ran in to find water all over the bathroom floor and a scroll sitting on the seat of the toilet. The scroll was, somehow, quite dry. It was tied with a light blue ribbon.

Tom's mother looked at the mess. "First the coffee table, then the telly – now this," she said with a sigh. "These challenges are getting pretty expensive. Do the Lords of Pain have any idea how much a decent plumber costs these days?"

She opened the scroll and read out the words inside, translating them from Japanese. Tom, meanwhile, mopped the floor and tidied up the chunks of broken toilet tank.

"The duel's in Germany," she said. "By a lake in the Black Forest. Near Baden-Baden."

"I've heard of Baden-Baden," said Tom.

"You have? Glad to see you've been paying attention in geography."

"Yeah, well, that and they held the World Cup there a few years back. It's a tourist town, right? Posh shops and restaurants. The footballers' wives loved it. But it's a funny name."

"I think it means 'bath-bath'. There are hot springs there, and the water's good for your health. Like in Bath in England."

"But with twice as much bath," said Tom. "So, when's the duel supposed to start?"

"Sunday," said Tom's mother. "Early morning."

Tom thought about Natalie's party. He wouldn't be able to go. Damn.

Then he remembered.

He *could* go. Because he wasn't the Contest champion now.

"Are we going to tell Mai and Akiko about this?" he said.

"Do you think we should?" said his mother.

"I don't know how else they're going to find out."

"I'm pretty sure Akiko will be able to figure it out for herself. I've called her a witch,

87

haven't I? Well, I'm not kidding about that. She has powers."

"Such as taking control of the Shinobi Ghosts," said Tom.

"Yes," said his mother. "But that's the least of it. Your father used to joke about her. He'd say, *I love Akiko-san very much and I tell her so all the time. She'd turn me into a frog if I didn't.* Only, I don't think it was meant to be a joke."

"Come to think of it, it is pretty spooky how she got into my hospital room in the middle of the night," Tom said. "No one's allowed to stay in a hospital at night except patients and staff."

Jane Yamada nodded. "I think Akiko already knows where the duel's taking place."

"But," said Tom, "what if she doesn't?"

"You'd like me to phone her and tell her, wouldn't you?"

"Could you? Just to be on the safe side."

"I really don't want to," Tom's mother said. "But for your sake, I will."

Jane Yamada made a whole lot of phone calls. She didn't have a number for Great-aunt Akiko, but she still had contacts among the Yamada family in Japan. At last she got through to Akiko. They had a short talk in Japanese. Tom watched his mother speaking on the phone and saw disgust in her face. For her, talking to Akiko was like cleaning up a blocked-up drain. A horrid and messy task.

She was happy when the call was over.

"She did know already," she told Tom. "She was very polite and nice. She thanked me for being kind enough to inform her about the duel but she said she had everything under control. She also said how glad she was to meet you in Tokyo, Tom, and what a charming boy you were. She praised me for bringing you up so well." Jane Yamada gave a shudder. "You know how when a spider catches a fly, it wraps it up in web silk first, before sinking its fangs in? That's how I felt. Just like that fly. Being tied up, waiting for the poison to be injected into me."

"Anyway, it's over now," said Tom.

"Yes." His mother gave a long sigh. "We've done what we had to do. That's that. Any idea what you're up to today?"

"I was planning on doing nothing."

"Good. It's always good to have a plan."

All that Friday, Tom tried not to think about the duel. And that night, he lay in bed also trying not to think about the duel. And the following morning, he was still trying not to think about the duel.

He was trying not to think about it even as he left the house at 6 a.m. on Saturday morning. He was carrying a backpack. He took the tube to Waterloo Station, and, all the way, he did his best to keep the duel far from his thoughts.

On the Eurostar train to Paris, Tom stared out of the window, watching England rush by, then France. The duel was on his mind but not *in* it.

From Paris, he took another train to Berlin. The duel? What duel?

At Berlin he boarded yet another train, which carried him south across Germany. Duel? No.

It was late at night when Tom reached Baden-Baden. He'd written a note before leaving the house, telling his mother where he had gone. Now he texted her to tell her he'd got there safely.

His mother's reply was sharp.

U R an idiot. It's *not* ur fight any more. Leave it alone.

But Tom couldn't leave it alone. He just couldn't.

He found a hotel, one that looked cheap but clean. He had used his mother's credit card to pay for all those train tickets. He had spent a lot of money on them. His mother would grumble when the bill came, but he knew she would pay it off. She always did.

He lay on the bed, thinking that right now he could be at Natalie's house, hanging out with Debbie. He hadn't rung Debbie to tell her he wasn't going to the party. He didn't have her phone number, for one thing, although he could have got hold of it if he'd wanted to. He had the number of one of her friends, whom he was kind of friends with.

The truth was, Tom had been scared to get in touch with Debbie. He hadn't wanted to let her down by saying he couldn't make it to the party. She would have asked him why, and he'd have had to come up with some lame excuse, which she would have seen through easily.

It was better if he just didn't turn up.

"Yeah," he said to himself. "Much better to do that. So much more cool."

He set the alarm on his phone for 4 a.m. Then he slept.

Just after sunrise, a taxi collected him and drove him through Baden-Baden. Tom looked out at the still-sleeping town. The houses were brightly painted, with shutters on the windows and with steep pointed roofs. There were squares filled with trees, and market-places, and bars, lots of bars. Everything seemed very neat and tidy, as if a crowd of maid-servants came through every day, cleaning up the town and sweeping away every last speck of dust.

"To the Mummelsee, yes?" the taxi driver said.

"Yes."

"For the hiking?"

"Yes," said Tom. "To do a bit of hiking."

"The Mummelsee," said the driver. "A beautiful lake. But there is a mystery. There is an old story about a king who lives there under the water. He drags maidens down into his kingdom to be his wives. Also, mermaids and water sprites live in the lake. They try to catch you and drown you. A place to avoid, if you believe these things. But there has been real danger there lately. A bad thing happened, just yesterday. It was ... I am not sure of the word. When the ground falls? You know? Part of the hill comes down? Like this, *crash*."

"A landslide?" Tom said.

The driver smacked the steering wheel. "Yes! So! Landslide. It has been raining very hard here for two, three days. The ground is wet and soft. So it happens. The earth gives way. Landslide. Many trees come down.

Police say the area is still not safe. They say stay away please. They make people leave all the houses and hotels near the lake. But you look like a sensible boy. I think you will be careful up there, no?"

"I'll try," Tom said.

The road led out of Baden-Baden. It snaked higher and higher into the hills. Soon the taxi was driving through the Black Forest. Pine trees towered on both sides. Their branches let very little sunlight through. The air was thick with mist and shadows.

The taxi driver let Tom out beside a sign that read "Mummelsee – 1.5km". The sign pointed to a footpath that wound uphill through the trees.

"Enjoy the hiking, my friend!" the driver said, and the taxi roared away.

Tom set off along the footpath.

Chapter 10
A Meeting in the Forest

A few birds flitted from tree to tree. The wind whispered in the tops of the pines. Squirrels scurried over the carpet of dead needles. The smell of the trees was very strong. Tom slogged uphill through the dense shadows, feeling that he must be the only human being for miles around.

All at once he was in day-light again and the Mummelsee came into sight. The lake's surface glinted in the early morning sunshine. Hills sloped steeply all round it, and Tom could see where the landslide had happened. The side of one of the hills looked as if a huge hand had reached down and scooped away a large section. The soil was laid bare, and fallen trees lay at the bottom of the hill in a jumble.

The duel would be taking place somewhere near that spot. The landslide would keep people away. No humans should attend the Contest unless they were meant to be there.

Tom walked round the lake's edge towards the duel site. He was nearly there when a figure stepped out from between two trees, blocking his way.

Tom stopped still. His heart was thumping.

"Holy cow!" he yelled. "You gave me a shock. What are you doing here?"

"I could ask you the same question, Tom," said Dragon, with a dry smile. "I thought you'd had it with the Contest. I thought you'd given up. And yet here you are."

"Yes, well," said Tom. He looked down at his feet. "I thought so too. But I needed to come. I just ... had to. In order to be sure. I mean, what if Mai couldn't make it? What if her plane was held up or, I don't know, crashed into the sea?"

"And what if your own sense of duty wouldn't let you stay at home?" said Dragon.

"There's that too," said Tom.

"It's nothing to be ashamed of, Tom. A sense of duty is a noble thing. The fact is, I knew you'd be coming."

"You did?"

"Yes. Even before your mother phoned me yesterday and said you had crept out before she woke up. I knew, because I know you. I know how much honour you have. How much pride. You couldn't let somebody else fight your fight for you. That wouldn't be a Tom Yamada thing to do at all."

"Oh," said Tom. He felt pleased. He also felt bad. He'd left Tokyo without telling Dragon. Without even saying goodbye. All because of that thing with Dragon's eyes, that flash of fire which might have happened or not. Because of that and the row they'd had.

But now all Tom could think was that Dragon was his *sensei*. His teacher. A man he feared but also had great respect for.

A man who, deep down, cared for him. This was clear to Tom now. Why else would Dragon be here? Why else would he say what he'd just said? Dragon cared for him and even had respect for him.

Tom made a fist of one hand and placed the knuckles against the open palm of his other hand. He bowed to Dragon.

"*Sensei*," he said. "I'm sorry."

"I know," said Dragon, bowing back to Tom. "I know something else as well. You've come without any weapons, haven't you?"

Tom gave a nod, looking ashamed. "I brought a few *shuriken*. That's all I had at home."

"Well, it just so happens that you're in luck," Dragon said. He pointed to a large sports bag lying next to a nearby tree. "I have everything you need right here."

Chapter 11
The Lord of Tears

The duel site was in an open space within the forest, close to the edge of the landslide. The gateway to the arena filled the space between two tree trunks. It hung there like a sheet of shimmering mist.

Tom walked quickly through it into the arena. Now the trees on all sides were ugly, dark things. The pines of the Black Forest had been tall and upright. These trees, however, were low and bent and twisted, as though they had been tortured by some unseen hand.

Demons sat in the branches and clung to the trunks with their claws.

They had come to see the duel. But Tom didn't notice either the trees or the demons. He was looking at what was going on in the middle of the arena.

The duel had already begun.

Tom recalled Dragon telling him that no living creature could pass through one of the white gateways into the demons' world, except a Yamada. Mai was a Yamada. And now she was here, locked in a fierce battle with the Lord of Tears.

The Lord of Tears was a giant, at least twelve feet tall. He was naked except for a cloth around his loins, and his skin was shiny blue and had a kind of rubbery look about it. He moved like lightning. Tom had never seen anything so fast. The Lord of Tears dashed about the arena, running round and round Mai. He didn't so much travel from one place to another as *flow*. One leg would stretch out, getting longer and longer and thinner and thinner like a piece of bubble gum. It would plant its foot on the spot where it wanted to be. Then the rest of the Lord of Tears would snap over to that spot in an instant. He would hit Mai the moment he got there. She would spin round to strike back, but she was never quite fast enough. The Lord of Tears would be off to somewhere else before she could get a fix on where he was.

Mai was armed with a pair of *katana*. She whirled the swords about her in flickering silver circles. But as far as Tom could tell, she hadn't yet been able to cut the Lord of Tears. Not even a tiny nick on his skin.

The Lord of Tears, on the other hand, was unarmed, but he was still winning the duel with Mai. His punches, slaps and kicks came at her from all sides. Tom saw him cuff her round the head. Next moment, he booted her in the backside. The moment after that, he jabbed her in the arm with his fingers.

Mai stayed up on her feet. The Lord of Tears gave her blow after blow but she kept standing. She also kept lashing out with the two *katana*. She was holding her ground, despite the endless attack from the Lord of Tears. He was showing no mercy. Tom was impressed.

But Tom got the clear sense that the Lord of Tears was just toying with Mai. He was playing with her like a cat with a mouse. The big grin on the arch-demon's face told Tom that. So did the cruel gleam in his glowing red eyes.

"They sent a girl?" the Lord of Tears said, howling with laughter. "They sent a *girl* to do the job of a man? How stupid can they be?"

Mai's mouth was tight. She must try to win. She slashed at her enemy again and again, missing again and again but never giving up.

At last it seemed that the Lord of Tears had had enough of playing. He zipped round behind Mai and grabbed her hands. He raised them high, so that the swords were out of harm's way. Mai squirmed in his grasp. She kicked backwards, but the Lord of Tears simply arched his body out of the way. He was tall enough and flexible enough to do this.

"Little girl," he said with a snarl, "you are no champion. You fight well, I'll grant you that. But I have known true champions. You have great skills. Your style is fantastic. But you do not have heart – and a warrior without heart is no warrior at all. I've enjoyed this little scuffle of ours. It was a pleasant workout. But now, I'm afraid, it's over, and we must part."

He lifted Mai off the ground, as if she were as light as a feather. Then he yanked her arms out to the sides.

"Or rather," the Lord of Tears said, "*you* must part. As in, your arms must part from their sockets."

He began to pull Mai's arms away from her body.

Mai twisted and screamed.

That was when Tom stepped forward, drawing his *katana* from its sheath.

"Put her down!" he shouted.

The Lord of Tears turned his head.

"Ah, there you are," he said. "The real Yamada. I was not sure when you were going to show up. As a matter of fact, I was wondering *if* you were going to show up at all."

"T-Tom," gasped Mai.

"Put her down," Tom repeated. "Your duel is with me, not her. I'm the Contest champion. Let her go, and fight me."

The Lord of Tears looked down at Mai. "But we're having so much fun, she and I," he said. "Can you wait just a minute till I've finished tearing her to little bloody pieces?"

Tom waved his *katana* in the air.

"Now," he said.

The Lord of Tears stuck out his lower lip like a spoilt child. "Oh, very well," he said. He dumped Mai onto the ground, plucking her swords from her hands as he did so.

Mai gave a groan.

"Go," Tom said to her. "I've got this. Go on, go!"

Mai limped off to the edge of the arena. She didn't seem too badly hurt. She seemed ashamed, more than anything. All her life she'd been getting ready to take part in a duel like this. And now that her chance had come, she'd failed.

Tom turned to face the Lord of Tears.

"You and me, big guy," he said.

The Lord of Tears twirled Mai's two *katana*.

"Time to die, Yamada," he said.

Chapter 12
Patterns

Tom had seen something while watching Mai and the Lord of Tears fight.

The Lord of Tears had moved in a circle round Mai. He'd always put his right leg out first. This was known as "leading" with that leg. So he'd always been moving anti-clockwise round Mai.

Dragon had taught Tom to look for patterns like this in an enemy's fighting style. He'd also taught Tom to try and avoid having patterns in his own style.

"Patterns make it easy for your enemy to know what you will do next," he'd said. "Patterns must be broken. Otherwise your enemy will break them for you – to your cost."

Now, as Tom and the Lord of Tears faced off against each other, Tom saw that the arch-demon was still leading with his right leg. He was moving to his right, holding one *katana* up in the air and the other out in front.

"You've won two duels," the Lord of Tears said. "You've sent the Lord of the Mountain back to his castle in the snowy peaks, and the Lord of the Void home to his gloomy cavern. You're not the pushover we were expecting you to be, that much is clear. Even at just fifteen years old, you've proved yourself a great warrior. But, Yamada, the odds are truly stacked against you this time. I am faster than you. I am taller than you. I have one more sword than you. What do you have that I don't have?"

"Clothes, for one thing," Tom said. "Look at you. Aren't you cold like that?"

The Lord of Tears looked down at his own near-naked body.

Tom sprang at him. His *katana* whirred through the air.

Blades clashed.

"Oh, very nice," said the Lord of Tears. He had blocked Tom's strike, with his two swords crossed in an X-shape. "Distracting me, making me look down. But you don't seem to have grasped just how fast I am."

The Lord of Tears swung both his *katana* at Tom from either side. Tom ducked one of them and blocked the other with his own *katana*. But it was a close thing. He'd hardly seen the swords move, and the one that passed above his head missed by a millimetre or two. He felt it whizz across the top of his hair, like a breeze.

111

Tom took two steps forward, with his sword raised at eye-level. He had to stay on the attack and make the Lord of Tears defend himself. He must go at him. He couldn't risk another two-sword strike from his enemy. Just because he'd survived one, it didn't mean he would survive another.

He thrust his *katana* at the arch-demon's navel.

But the Lord of Tears evaded him. He did one of those swift, flowing side-steps – to his right, of course. In the blink of an eye, he was standing on Tom's left.

Tom turned his sword through 90 degrees. He stabbed left with it.

But the Lord of Tears wasn't there any more. He was standing right behind Tom.

Tom had to leap out of range fast. He did a forward roll. He came up on his feet, and spun round.

The Lord of Tears strode towards him.

"Ducking, diving, rolling ..." he said. "You must be good in the gym. But I wonder how long you can keep it up."

He ran at Tom.

There wasn't time to think. All Tom could do was fling himself flat on the ground.

The Lord of Tears was going so fast, he overshot. He ran right over the top of Tom.

Tom scrambled to his feet. He wheeled round.

The Lord of Tears was ten metres away. Then, with a sudden blur of movement, he was straight in front of Tom. Both of his *katana* came down side by side in a parallel strike. Tom was lucky. His own sword happened to be horizontal. He just managed to block the double blow.

The Lord of Tears was on Tom's left-hand side.

The Lord of Tears was behind Tom.

The Lord of Tears was on Tom's right.

He slashed at Tom each time. Tom whirled in a frenzy, trying to keep up with the Lord of Tears and block his attacks. He began to feel dizzy.

The Lord of Tears was following his pattern – a step to the right every time. Tom had to use it against him somehow.

Then Tom recalled that Dragon had slipped a special kind of weapon into his pocket when arming him a few minutes ago.

Dragon had given him some *tetsu-bishi*. These were twisted metal spikes. They looked a bit like the jacks from the game of ball and jacks, but larger and sharper. Ninjas used them to hurt enemies they were running away from. They would toss the *tetsu-bishi* behind them and their enemies would step on the *tetsu-bishi* if they didn't see them in time. The spikes could go through the soles of shoes. If you trod on one, you wouldn't be running again for a long while.

Tom snatched a handful of the *tetsu-bishi* from his pocket. He hurled them onto the ground in front of him, on the spot where he knew the Lord of Tears would step onto next.

The Lord of Tears hadn't seen this. He stretched out his right leg and placed his bare foot down, right on top of the *tetsu-bishi*.

He screamed.

It was Tom's chance. The Lord of Tears was rooted to the spot, unable to move with the sudden pain.

Tom jabbed his *katana* out in front of him.

The Lord of Tears looked down at himself.

"Oh," he said.

Tom's *katana* was stuck into the base of the arch-demon's belly, just above the groin.

Tom yanked the sword out and thrust it in again. Blood spattered the ground both behind and in front of the Lord of Tears.

Tom ran him through with the sword a third time.

The Lord of Tears choked. His jaw gaped open. He looked down at Tom, puzzled.

"Sneaky," he gasped.

"Sneaky as a snake," Tom said. He shoved the *katana* upwards as high as he could reach. He sliced through the arch-demon's belly muscles. Guts spilled out, hot and steaming.

The Lord of Tears fell to the ground with a scream and a gurgle. His body shuddered and shook. At last he stopped moving.

Chapter 13

Shame

Mai walked out of the arena with Tom, through the misty gateway. She couldn't look him in the eye.

Back in the forest – the proper Black Forest – Dragon took Tom's *katana*. He also took the blue Element Gem, which Tom had dug out of the heart of the Lord of Tears as he lay on the ground.

Dragon looked at Mai. "You must be Tom's cousin."

"I am nothing," Mai said in a bitter voice. "I am no one. I'm a disgrace to the Yamada family."

"Not so," said Dragon. "To judge by the state of you – you're called Mai, right?"

Mai nodded.

"To judge by the state of you, Mai, you fought the Lord of Tears. Is that so?"

"It is."

"Then you were very brave. You stood up to one of the Five Lords of Pain. There is no disgrace in that. Disgrace would lie in not entering the arena in the first place."

"Really?" Mai raised her head. Hope shone in her eyes. "So I didn't fail?"

Dragon gave her a smile. "You didn't. To lose in combat is not to fail. To fail is not to take part, not to be brave enough." His smile grew cold. "But still, you should not have been here. There is someone else here who has brought disgrace on the Yamada family."

Dragon swung round, peering into the trees.

"And that someone is *you*, Akiko Umari," he said. "Oh, yes, don't think I didn't see you hiding there. You and your two friends."

Great-aunt Akiko stepped into view from behind the trunk of one of the tallest, thickest pines. She had a pair of Shinobi Ghosts with her, as she had had at the hospital. She was all hunched up and looked angry.

"Do I know you?" she asked Dragon. "*Should* I know you?"

"There is no reason why you should ever have heard of a man like me, Akiko-san," said Dragon.

Tom could hear the rude note in Dragon's voice as he used the polite name for Great-

119

aunt Akiko. In truth, Dragon was being anything but polite to her.

"I am just a humble martial arts teacher," Dragon went on. "I run a small *dojo* in London. Your granddaughter Mai called herself *no one* just now, but I truly am no one. You, on the other hand, have a great and far-reaching reputation. You are a very well-known lady, respected by all, and I, Dragon, am as far beneath your notice as an ant is beneath an elephant's."

"Hmph," said Great-aunt Akiko. She studied Dragon with her spidery eyes, moving her head from side to side. "I don't know whether to be pleased or insulted. It is plain to all that you do not mean what you say. But I see something else in you, too. Something more. Something deeper. I do not know what it is."

She seemed confused, Tom thought. And he could tell that Great-aunt Akiko was someone who didn't like feeling confused.

"Madam," said Dragon. "I've no doubt that you meant well when you put your granddaughter up to become a Contest champion, even though she has no right to claim that title. I've no doubt that your motives were pure. You wished to be sure that the Contest was in safe hands and that our side had the best possible chance of victory."

"That is true," said Great-aunt Akiko. "And – "

Dragon broke in here. "But," he said, "your plan nearly led to disaster."

"How dare you speak when I am – "

"You put the outcome of the Contest in danger," Dragon carried on, taking no notice of Great-aunt Akiko's protest. "You caused the true champion, Tom, to step aside from the path of his fate." His voice rose. "You are an evil little toad who insists on getting her own way. If you have any sense of dignity you will leave right now. Take your granddaughter and

your Shinobi Ghosts with you. And never –
never – meddle with this Contest again. Do
you understand me?"

Tom fought hard to keep a grin from his
face. Dragon had really stuck it to Great-aunt
Akiko. The nasty little woman had had it
coming, too.

Great-aunt Akiko was white with rage. She
was shaking all over. She sucked in her lips so
tightly, that her mouth almost vanished.

At last she said, "This is not over. This is
far from over."

"Oh, I think it is," said Dragon.

"I will learn more about you, Dragon,"
Great-aunt Akiko said. "I will find out all there
is to know about you. And I will use what I
learn against you. You wait and see. You have
insulted me. I shall not forget that. I will
punish you. Mai!" She beckoned to her

granddaughter with one claw-like hand.
"Come. It is time for us to go."

Mai took a step towards her grandmother.
Then she stopped and turned to Tom.

"Tomeo-san," she said, and she bowed her
head low to him.

Tom was taken aback. But he returned the
bow.

"You did what I could not do," Mai said.
"The Lord of Tears was right. I do not have
heart. I am not a true warrior. You are."

"Er, thanks," said Tom. "That means
something, coming from you."

Mai smiled shyly. "I hope we shall meet
again some time ... cousin."

"Yeah," said Tom. "I hope so too."

"Mai!" snapped Great-aunt Akiko.

Mai trotted over to her. She, Akiko and the two Shinobi Ghosts strode off into the forest, and were soon lost from sight.

Tom turned to Dragon.

"Nice one," he said. "Akiko deserved that. But aren't you worried? I don't think she makes empty threats."

Dragon's orange-brown eyes were hard and amused.

"I've heard worse," he said. "People like Akiko, they do indeed have power. But mostly they would rather not use it. They prefer talk and bluster. It costs them less."

"You're not even just a tiny bit scared?"

"I'd like to think," Dragon said, "that there's nothing Akiko Umari can do to me that I can't do to her. I'd like to think she knows it too."

Tom couldn't quite make sense of this remark. Maybe it was just a boast.

"All right," he said with a shrug. "If you say so."

Dragon dug into his pocket and took out the Element Gem. "This is yours, by the way," he said. "I don't see why I should have to carry it home."

Tom slipped the gem into his own pocket. He'd handed it to Dragon for him to look at, but really it was *his* prize, wasn't it?

Dragon picked up the sports bag.

"Lovely morning for a stroll through the woods," he said, and he and Tom set off along the path that led back to the road.

List of Japanese Words

Akiko: female name; it means either "autumn child" or "bright child"

Hanbo: pole with a blade at either end, usually about 1 metre long

Hoko: pole made of bamboo with a three-pointed blade at the tip

Kanji: Japanese writing

Kata: pattern of movements used for learning and practising martial arts

Katana: long sword used by warriors, such as the samurai (see picture)

Konnichiwa: "good afternoon", "good evening" in Japanese

Mai: female name; it means "dance"

Manriki-gusari: length of iron chain at least one metre long, with weights on both ends (see picture)

Ninja-to: short sword used by ninjas

Sayonara: Japanese for "goodbye"

Sensei *(sen-say)*: polite name for a master or teacher

Shinobi: another word for ninja

Shuriken: a throwing-star made of iron (see picture)

Tanto: 30-centimetre-long dagger

Tetsu-bishi: small metal spikes for throwing at your enemy's feet

Tomeo: Tom's full name; in Japanese it means "man who takes no risks"

Check out Tom's next duel in ...

The Lord of the Typhoon

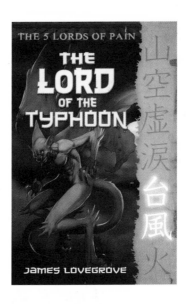

Tom faces the Lord of the Typhoon – the winged monster that killed Tom's father. Can Tom get his revenge?

Turn the page to read the start of the next book!

Camden Market

Tom Yamada had battled demons.

He'd faced zombie ninjas.

He'd gone head-to-head with his own cousin, Mai, who was more skilled in martial arts than anyone else in Japan.

But one thing truly scared him, and that was meeting Debbie Williams again.

Tom had been keeping out of Debbie's way for more than a month, ever since she'd asked him out to that party and he'd stood her up. It was the summer holidays, so he hadn't had to worry about sitting near Debbie in class or seeing her at lunch at school. However, she didn't live very far from where Tom did. He knew their paths were going to cross, sooner or later. And he wasn't looking foward to it at all.

In the end they met on a baking hot day in August. Tom had gone down to Camden Market to pick up some cheap games for his console. There was a stall at the market that sold them second-hand. Jaz, the stall owner, sometimes had beta-test versions of brand new games as well. It was against the law, but it was a good way of getting hold of the latest platform games and shoot-'em-ups long before they went on sale in the proper shops.

"Tom?"

Tom had been wandering head down through the market, lost in thought. He looked up at the sound of his name.

It was Debbie Williams who'd spoken to him. Debbie was with two other girls. One was Natalie Bennett, who'd given the party Tom didn't go to. The other was someone Tom didn't know. Between the three of them they were holding at least twenty carrier bags. A massive girly clothes-shopping spree.

"Oh, er, Debbie," said Tom. "Hi." All at once he was feeling about three feet tall. His heart was thudding in his ears. He wished he could be somewhere else, anywhere so long as it wasn't here.

Natalie was frowning at him. Debbie was looking at him as if he was a bit of a mystery to her. There was a hint of sadness in her eyes, too.

"You got something nice, then?" she said.

"Huh?"

"That." Debbie pointed at Tom's paper bag. "Something nice?"

So they were to have a polite chat. That was how Debbie wanted to play it, did she?

"Um, yeah," Tom said. "It's a present. For my friend Sharif. You know him. From school. Sharif Khan. Him with the bushy eyebrows. Good at science."

"I know who Sharif is," Debbie said. "Everyone does. He's the one who got attacked. Knifed in the street outside his house. Poor thing. The police still haven't found who did it, have they?"

"And they never will," Tom said, without thinking.

Barrington Stoke would like to thank all its readers for commenting on the manuscript before publication and in particular:

Lizzie Alder
Richard Brant
Polly Byrne
Josh Caddy
Andrew Campbell
Mary Campbell
John Cowe
Ryan Crowle
Brandon Ellis
George Evans
Jake Francis
Robert Garside
Susan Gillespie
CJ Lethbridge
Tré Pusey
Sam Quarterman
Caroline Rowse
Rachael Sargent
Haydn Smallwood
Martisha Thompson
Jordan Truscott

Become a Consultant!

Would you like to be a consultant? Ask your parent, carer or teacher to contact us at the email address below – we'd love to hear from them! They can also find out more by visiting our website.

schools@barringtonstoke.co.uk
www.barringtonstoke.co.uk